PEANUTS®

SNOOPY Goes to School

By Charles M. Schulz
Written by Jason Cooper
Illustrated by Robert Pope

SIMON SPOTLIGHT
New York London Toronto Sydney New Delhi

SIMON SPOTLIGHT
An imprint of Simon & Schuster Children's Publishing Division
1230 Avenue of the Americas, New York, New York 10020
This Simon Spotlight paperback edition June 2020

For information about special discounts for bulk purchases, please contact Simon & Schuster Special Sales
at 1-866-506-1949 or business@simonandschuster.com.
Manufactured in the United States of America 0520 LAK
2 4 6 8 10 9 7 5 3 1
ISBN 978-1-5344-6456-8
ISBN 978-1-5344-6457-5 (eBook)

One afternoon Snoopy was resting on top of his doghouse when his stomach alarm started grumbling. He was hungry!

Unfortunately, Charlie Brown was nowhere to be found.

He must be at school, Snoopy thought. *Education is important, but so is my afternoon snack!*

When Charlie Brown came home, Snoopy approached him with a supper dish.

"I know you're hungry, Snoopy, but it's not dinnertime yet," Charlie Brown said.

Snoopy didn't want to give up yet, so he followed Charlie Brown inside the house.

"I better start on my homework," Charlie Brown said. "I have a true-or-false worksheet due tomorrow." He sat down at the kitchen table and got to work.

Snoopy watched curiously as Charlie Brown answered each question. *Interesting*, thought Snoopy. *We never had true-or-false assignments in dog obedience school. It was only "Sit or else!"*

With nothing to do until suppertime, Snoopy sat down beside Charlie Brown and began writing his own answers to the worksheet. *I usually work with a typewriter*, Snoopy thought, *but I'll see if I can write out some Ts and Fs.*

The next morning Charlie Brown noticed that Snoopy was following him to school. “What are you doing?” Charlie Brown asked. “I already gave you breakfast.”

Snoopy handed Charlie Brown the worksheet he had completed last night.

"I've heard of dogs eating homework, but never doing homework," Charlie Brown said, surprised. Then he smiled. "Come on, Snoopy. We might as well ask my teacher, Miss Othmar, how you did!"

When they got to school, however, Snoopy received bad news. "The principal says dogs aren't allowed on school grounds," Charlie Brown said. "He thinks you'll be too much

Snoopy couldn't believe it. He handed Charlie Brown a piece of paper.

"I don't think your passport can get you into school. I'm sorry, pal." Charlie Brown gave him a hug. "I'll see you at home, I guess." With that, Charlie Brown headed into class.

"I wish Snoopy could've stayed," Charlie Brown said to Linus. "After all, he did do his homework."

Linus had an idea. "What if you asked Miss Othmar if you could bring Snoopy for show-and-tell?"

Charlie Brown's face lit up. "That's a great idea!" he said.

Back at home Snoopy was feeling grumpy. He didn't understand why he couldn't go to school. *I'm not distracting,* he thought. *If anything, I'm charming! Well, it's their loss, not mine.*

After school Charlie Brown rushed home. “Guess what, Snoopy?” he exclaimed. “Miss Othmar said I can bring you for show-and-tell tomorrow. That means you can come to school with me!”

Wonderful! Snoopy thought. *Who wouldn’t want to learn all about me?*

The next day the students at school were excited to see Snoopy. It had been a long time since anyone brought something as much fun for show-and-tell.

"I brought a moldy piece of bread, but Snoopy makes it seem uninteresting," Pigpen said.

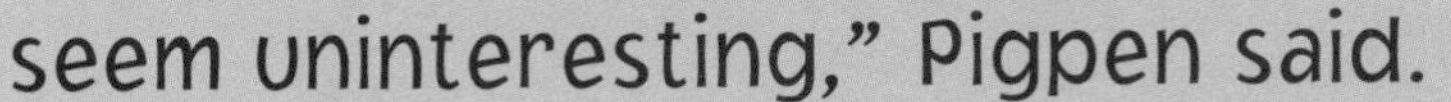

Charlie Brown stood proudly in front of the class. "For show-and-tell, I brought my dog, Snoopy."

Snoopy waved and bowed. Everyone waved back. The students asked a lot of questions. They wondered what it was like to take care of Snoopy.

"Taking care of a dog is a lot of fun," Charlie Brown began.

Then Snoopy cleared his throat loudly.

"Excuse me a moment, please," Charlie Brown told the class. He grabbed Snoopy's water dish from his backpack and filled it up at the water fountain in the hall. "Taking care of a dog is a lot of fun," he repeated, "but it's also a lot of work."

Snoopy cleared his throat again, offended.

"It's all worth it, though!" Charlie Brown added quickly.

"Snoopy has a great imagination," Charlie Brown continued.

Snoopy put on a scarf, helmet, and goggles.

"He really enjoys pretending he is a world-famous flying ace!" Charlie Brown added.

The class laughed.

What do you mean, pretending? Snoopy thought.

"Snoopy is smart and interesting," Charlie Brown said.

Snoopy started to dance and twirl around the room, making everyone cheer. No one was paying attention to Charlie Brown anymore.

". . . And bringing him here may turn out to be the biggest mistake of my life," he mumbled.

Snoopy, however, was having a wonderful day at school. He made new friends, played on the playground, and even discovered his favorite subject: lunch.

I'm beginning to understand why kids go to school every day, he thought.

After lunch Miss Othmar called Charlie Brown and Snoopy to her desk. As it turned out, Snoopy had received a perfect score on the true-or-false homework!

"He got every question right? But how?" Charlie Brown asked.

It's easy, Snoopy shrugged. *What's true is true, and what's false is false. . . .*

When the principal heard about Snoopy's perfect score, he called them into his office to ask questions.

"No, sir, I didn't help Snoopy on his homework," Charlie Brown said. "And he didn't cheat!"

The principal was not convinced, and Charlie Brown began to get nervous. "No, sir, I am not making fun of your school," he stammered.

Eventually, Charlie Brown and Snoopy were allowed to return to class. However, the principal made Charlie Brown promise never to let Snoopy do his homework for him.

"Good grief!" Charlie Brown said. "Now everyone thinks my dog is smarter than me!"

Still, overall it was a fun day at school. That night Charlie Brown served Snoopy a special dinner. “It was nice having you at school,” Charlie Brown said. “I guess your perfect score will always be a mystery.”

Snoopy nodded. *It sure will,* he thought. *I can’t even remember if the “T” stands for “true” or “false!”*